This book belongs to
....
....

Mademoiselle Gorilla

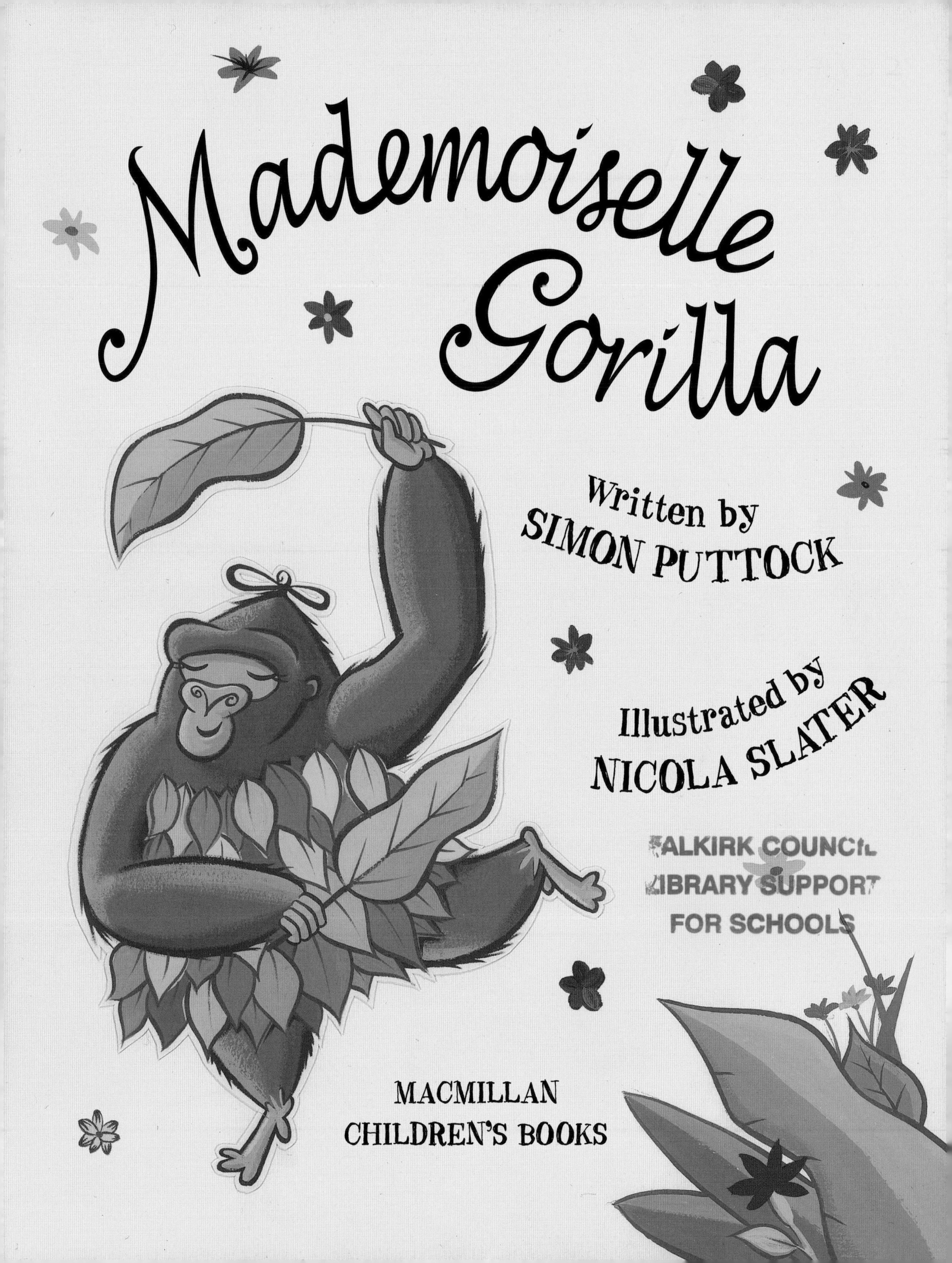

Written by
SIMON PUTTOCK

Illustrated by
NICOLA SLATER

MACMILLAN
CHILDREN'S BOOKS

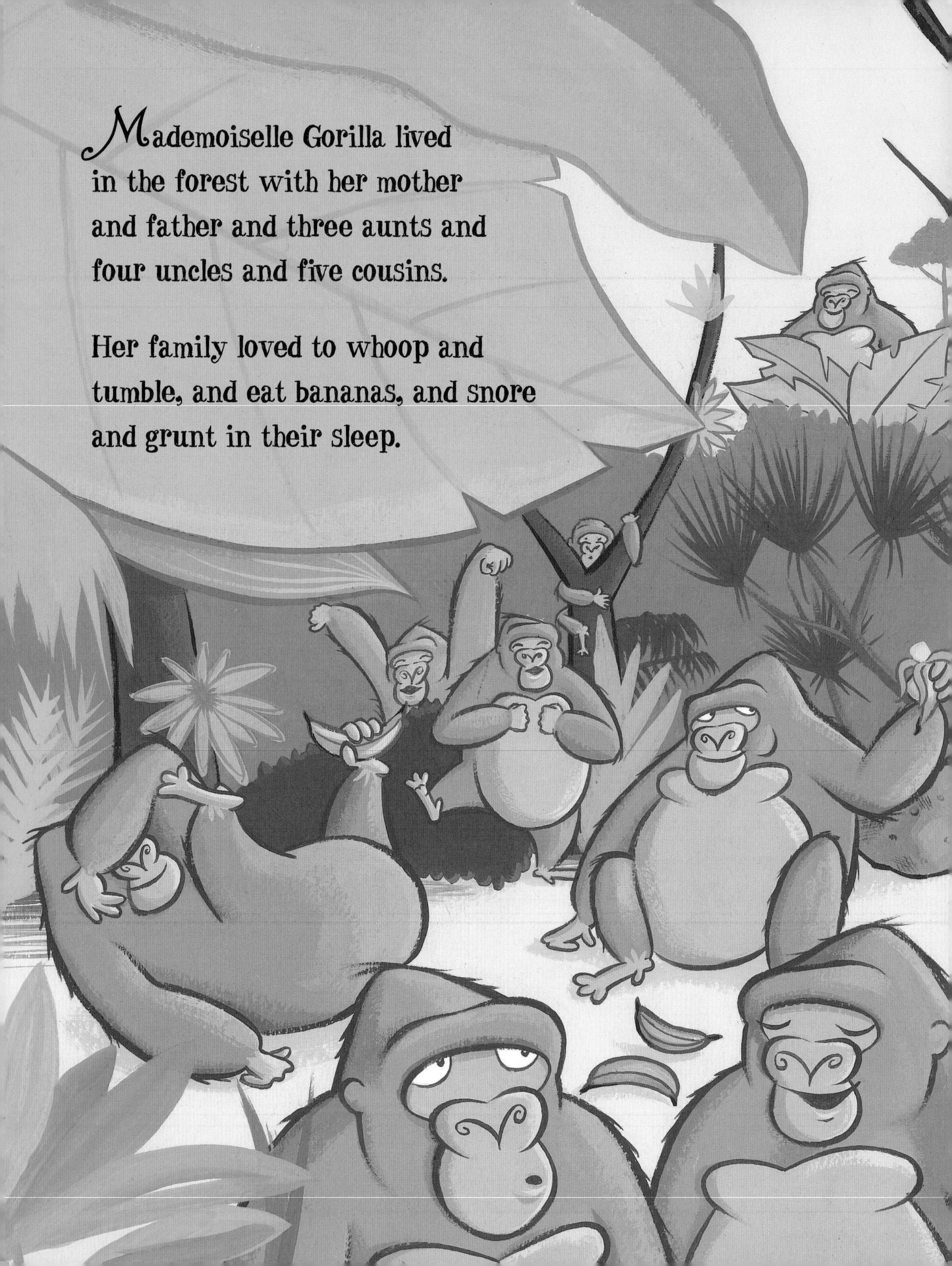

Mademoiselle Gorilla lived in the forest with her mother and father and three aunts and four uncles and five cousins.

Her family loved to whoop and tumble, and eat bananas, and snore and grunt in their sleep.

But Mademoiselle Gorilla was different.

"I do not grunt or snore.
I do not tumble or whoop," she said.
"I am a sensitive soul.
I have written a poem –

I wish that I could be, tra la,
a glamorous and dazzling star.
I feel it would be oh so fine
to be adorable and shine!"

Ho Ho!

"HOO HOO!" her family laughed. "That's so funny! Gorillas are hairy, not shiny. Hoo hoo!"

Hoo Hoo!

Hee Hee!

"But it is not **meant** to be funny, it is a poem,"

said Mademoiselle Gorilla crossly. "**You** are typical apes. **I** am a poet. And since I am not appreciated here, I will go somewhere where I shall be."

Ho Ho!

So Mademoiselle Gorilla made herself a dress of leaves and caught the boat to America.

The African Princess

In New York, Mademoiselle Gorilla recited her poem at smart parties.

She was a **great** success.

Everyone
shouted, "BRAVO!"
And, "What a charming dress!"
Soon, all the posh ladies were
wearing leafy dresses too!
And Mademoiselle Gorilla felt **appreciated.**

At one **very** smart party,
Mademoiselle Gorilla
was spotted by a famous
Hollywood film director.

"You are **adorable**," he said, "and I can make you a star. You **must** be in my next film."

It was another chance to shine. Mademoiselle Gorilla said, **"Yes please."**

So, bright and early
next morning,
she hopped
on a plane
to Hollywood.

"My dear," said the famous director, "please be a typical ape. Feel free to whoop and tumble, and eat bananas, and snore and grunt in your sleep."

"Well," said Mademoiselle Gorilla,
"I am **not** a typical ape,
I am really a poet, you know . . .

but I will do it, just this once."

When the film was finished, there was a glittery party.

Mademoiselle Gorilla felt like a star!

"I am glamorous," she thought. "I am dazzling and adored."

Gorilla
M. Gorilla

But . . .

when Mademoiselle Gorilla saw herself on the silver screen, being a **typical** ape, she thought longingly of the forest ... and her family ...

and she began to feel TERRIBLY homesick.

The famous director, however, was delighted. "I am a hit!" he cried.

"And you, Mademoiselle Gorilla, are a star. We will begin making another film at once."

To everyone's astonishment,
Mademoiselle Gorilla said, "No thank you."
"Nonsense!" cried the famous director.
"I can make you rich as well as a star."

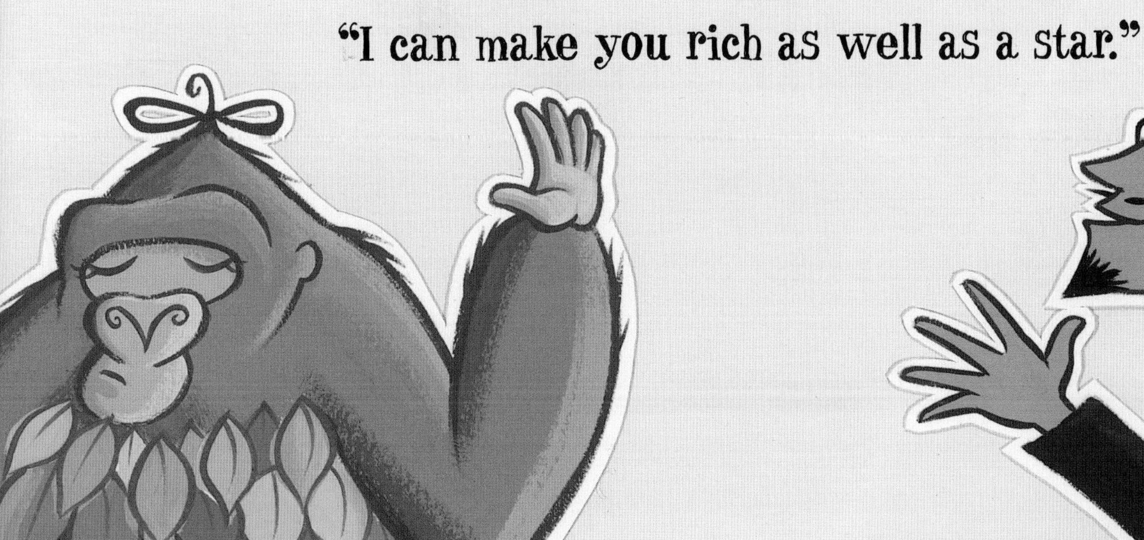

"Thank you again," said Mademoiselle,

"but no. Poets are seldom rich,
and gorillas, never.

It
is
time
for me
to go home."

Mademoiselle Gorilla's family were **ever** so pleased to have her back.

They did not know that she was now a famous poet and movie star. She was simply their very own Mademoiselle, and she had come home.

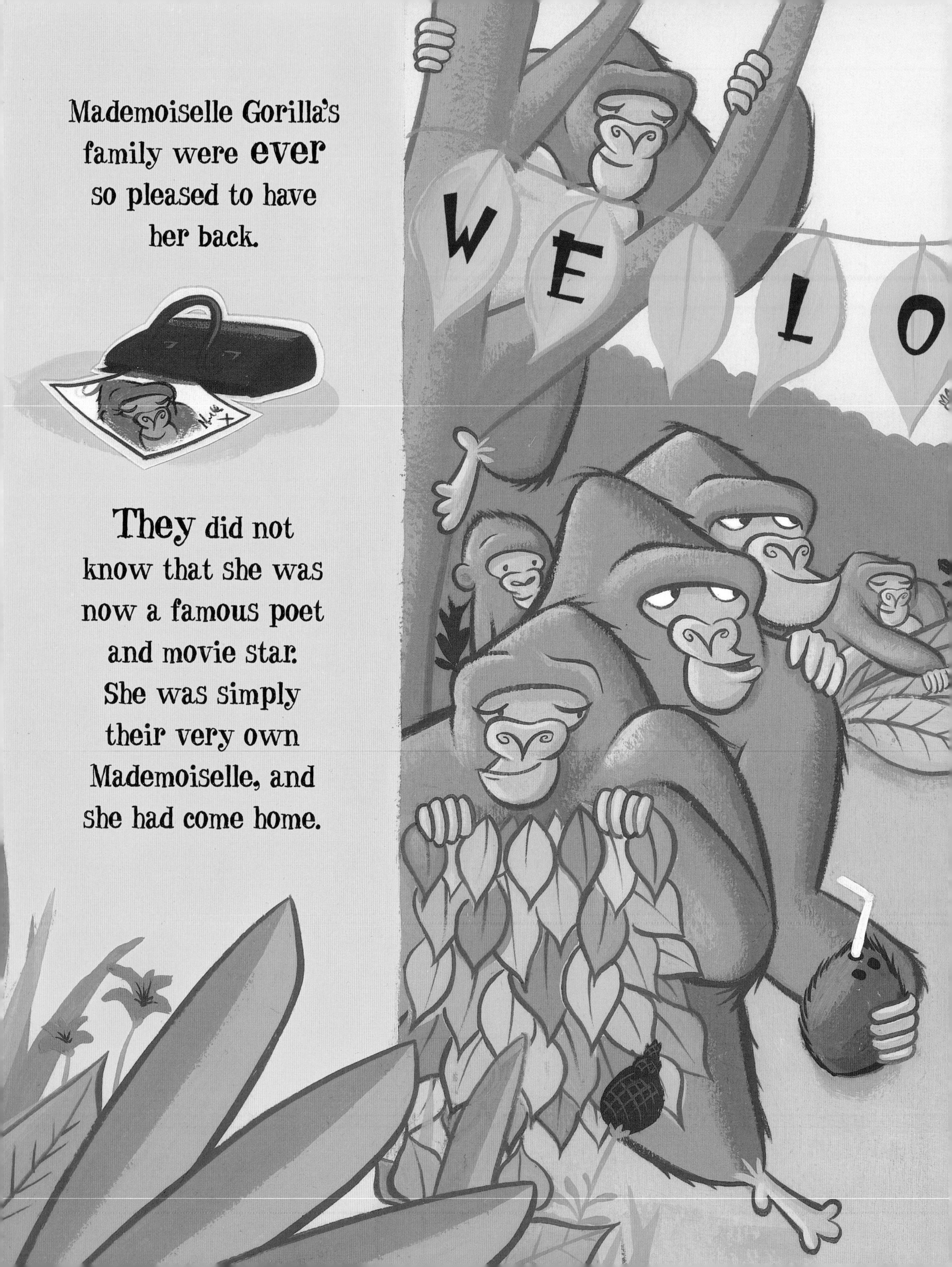

"Was it nice in America?" asked Mademoiselle Gorilla's mother.
"It was fabulous," said Mademoiselle, "but I did miss you all.
And I have written another poem – listen ...

"I know I'm very glamorous,
and you are all quite silly,
but we belong together,
love from Mademoiselle Gorilly!"

"HOO HOO!"
her family laughed.
"You're being funny again.
We do adore you."

And Mademoiselle Gorilla was happy, because now she knew that her family all appreciated her in their own special, gorillary way.

"You know what," she said.
"East or west, home's always best,
because I love you too.
And tonight I'm going to whoop it up,
because sometimes, that's what gorillas do."